Preacher &
The Tramp

**Written & Un-Edited
by Darick Spears**

FRESH OFF OF MY VACATION OF
THOUGHT,
NOW I AM HERE TO SERVE YOU
WITH A DEEP STORY.
SIMPLE,
YET COMPLEX..
STRAIGHT FORWARD,
YET SOMEWHAT LEFT FIELD.
BUT SOME WILL STILL CATCH MY
DRIFT.

HE WAS A RIGHTEOUS MAN IN THE
EYES OF THE PEOPLE,
A LEADER,
A SCHOLAR AND A GENTLEMAN.
YET UNDERNEATH HIS HEAVY
FLESH WAS A SAVAGE.
LUSTFUL,
ANGRY & BITTER MAN.

HE HATED HIS OWN REFLECTION,
UNSURE OF HOW TO ASSESS HIS
LUCK IN LIFE.
HE HAD A RICH LIFE,
MANY FRIENDS,
AND A BEAUTIFUL FAMILY.
A WIFE THAT LOVES HIM DEARLY,
AND KIDS WHO WORSHIPPED THE
GROUND HE WALKED ON.

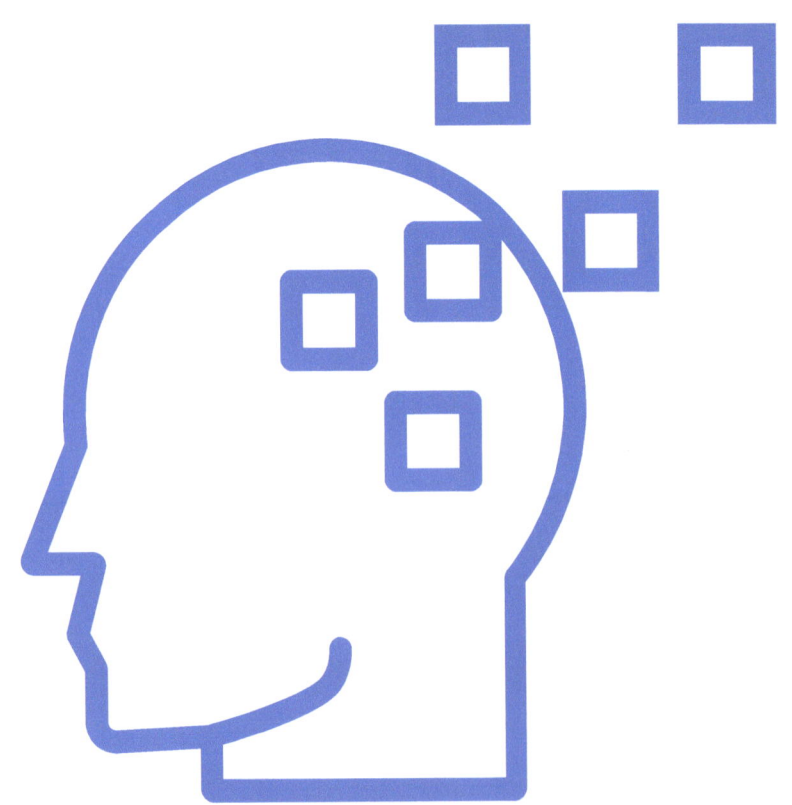

HOW COULD ANYONE LOVE ME?
HOW COULD I EVEN LOVE MYSELF?
THIS WAS THE THEME OF HIS DAILY PRAYER.
HOW COULD HE TEACH ANYONE ABOUT LIVING RIGHT --WHEN HIS LIFE WAS IMMERSED IN SINFUL FEELINGS?

One day the Preacher gave a
sermon to the people that got
the opposite reaction.
He admitted his faults,
His insecurities,
And how he felt so unworthy.

HE TALKED ABOUT HIS DAILY STRUGGLE WITH HIS FLESH.
HE CALLED HIS SERMON,
"PREACHER AND THE TRAMP"
HIS ANALOGY WAS BROKEN DOWN.
HE FELT THAT EVERYONE FIGHTS A WAR WITH RIGHTEOUSNESS VERSUS EVIL.

HIS PLAN WAS TO RETIRE AFTER
THIS HONEST SERMON,
BUT THE PEOPLE PRAISED HIM
FOR IT.
THEY LOVED IT SO MUCH THAT
THE DEMAND FOR HIM TO
PREACH WENT UP.
PEOPLE FOUND A DEEP
RELATABILITY AND COMPASSION
FOR HIS WALK WITH CHRIST.

INSTEAD OF RETIRING,
THIS PREACHER FOUND HIMSELF ON A WORLDWIDE STAGE.
GOD SPOKE TO HIM ONE NIGHT AND EXPLAINED TO HIM,
THAT IT WAS HIS HONESTY THAT SAVED HIM.
HIS HEART WAS PURE AND THE PEOPLE GOT A GLIMPSE TO SEE WHAT GOD HAD ALREADY KNOWN.

HIS SERMON "PREACHER AND THE TRAMP" BECAME A POPULAR MOVIE.

YEARS LATER IT WAS TURNED INTO A YEARLY CONFERENCE THAT HELPED MANY LOST SOULS FIND GOD.

HE WAS IN SUCH HIGH
DEMAND THAT HE FOUND
HIMSELF HAVING TO TURN
DOWN OFFERS.
HIS LIFE HAD CHANGED
TREMENDOUSLY FOR THE
BEST.

But one thing that never changed was his war with the flesh. Daily he had to deny the temptation. Women would throw themselves at him, and men.

As the pressure grew
stronger,
He found himself more
on his knees in prayer.
He was scared of
messing up.

THE PREACHER KNEW THAT
GOD HAS BLESSED HIM
IMMENSELY.
BUT SOMETIMES HIS DREAMS
WERE HUNTED BY DESIRES OF
BEAUTIFUL WOMEN,
AND HIS REALITY WOULD
SOMETIMES SEND HIM TO THE
BOTTLE.

DEPRESSED AND STRESSED OUT,
THE PREACHER FOUND HIMSELF IN
HIS OFFICE DRUNK.
HIS EYES FILLED WITH TEARS
BECAUSE HE FELT LIKE A FAILURE.

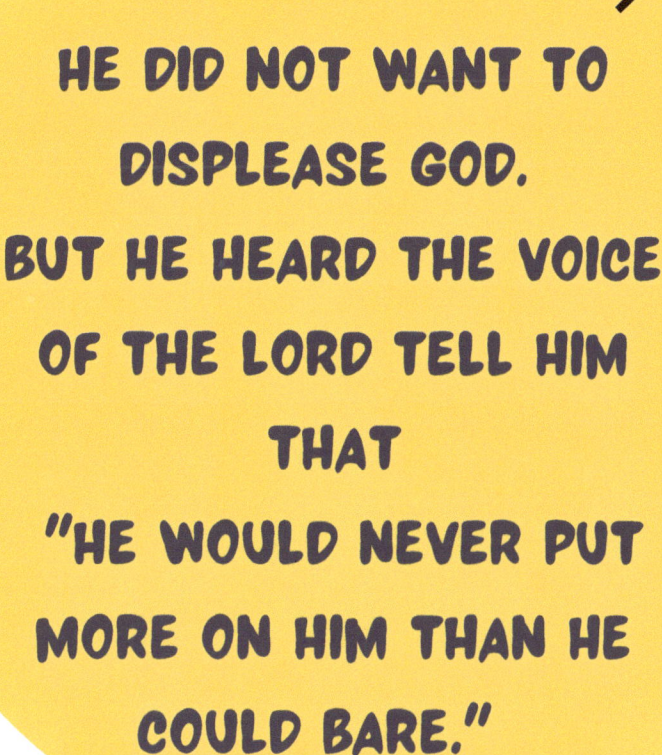

HE DID NOT WANT TO DISPLEASE GOD.
BUT HE HEARD THE VOICE OF THE LORD TELL HIM THAT
"HE WOULD NEVER PUT MORE ON HIM THAN HE COULD BARE."

THE PREACHER THEN REALIZED THAT HE HAD PUT MORE OF AN EXPECTATION ON HIMSELF THAN GOD HAD.

HE THEN REPENTED AND FOCUSED ON THE GOOD IN HIS LIFE.

HE WAS WORKING WITHIN HIS MINISTRY AND HELPING MILLIONS OF PEOPLE.

HE ALSO REALIZED THAT
HE SHOULDN'T STRESS OUT
OVER THE THINGS HE
COULD NOT CONTROL.
THE FLESH WILL ALWAYS
HAVE ITS DESIRES FOR AS
LONG AS WE DWELL IN IT.

THEREFORE, HAVING PUT AWAY FALSEHOOD, LET EACH ONE OF YOU SPEAK THE TRUTH WITH HIS NEIGHBOR, FOR WE ARE MEMBERS ONE OF ANOTHER.
EPHESIANS 4:25 ESV

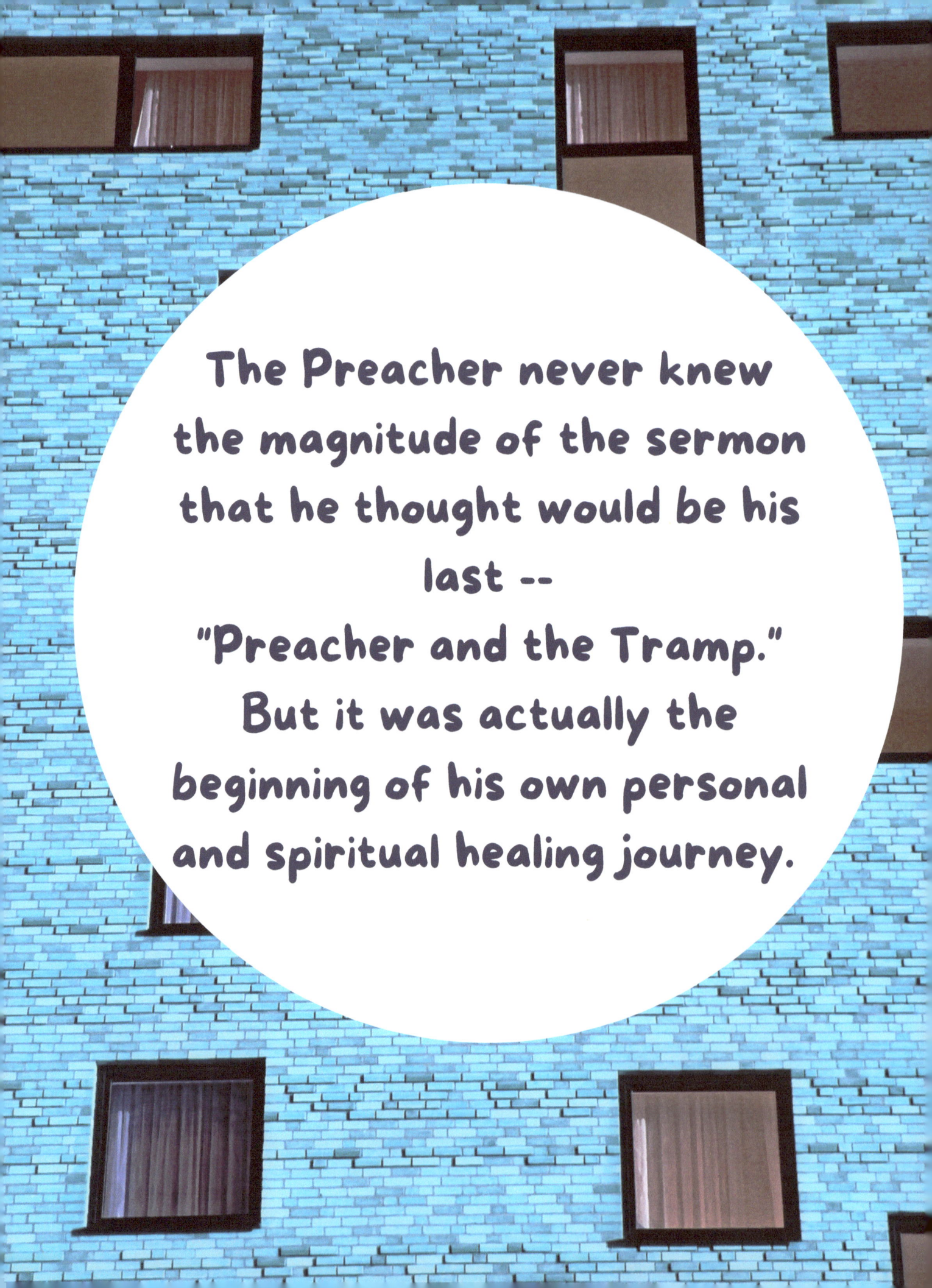

The Preacher never knew the magnitude of the sermon that he thought would be his last --
"Preacher and the Tramp."
But it was actually the beginning of his own personal and spiritual healing journey.

Preacher & The Tramp

BY DARICK SPEARS

Darick Books

THE FIRST BOOKSTORE OF ITS KIND